Whale, Quail, Snail

A Whale of a Tea Party

By Erica S. Perl

Illustrated by Sam Ailey

Ready-to-Read

Simon Spotlight

New York   London   Toronto   Sydney   New Delhi

To Charlotte, Audrey, and Rory — E. S. P.
For Jo and Donna — S. A.

SIMON SPOTLIGHT
An imprint of Simon & Schuster Children's Publishing Division
1230 Avenue of the Americas, New York, New York 10020
This Simon Spotlight edition December 2021
Text copyright © 2021 by Erica S. Perl
Illustrations copyright © 2021 by Sam Ailey
SIMON SPOTLIGHT, READY-TO-READ, and colophon are registered trademarks of
Simon & Schuster, Inc.
For information about special discounts for bulk purchases, please contact Simon &
Schuster Special Sales at 1-866-506-1949 or business@simonandschuster.com.
Manufactured in the United States of America 1021 LAK
2 4 6 8 10 9 7 5 3 1
This book has been cataloged by the Library of Congress.
ISBN 978-1-5344-9730-6 (hc)
ISBN 978-1-5344-9729-0 (pbk)
ISBN 978-1-5344-9731-3 (ebook)

Once upon a time, there was a whale named Whale.

Whale lived near Tiny Island.
Tiny Island had one palm tree,
one mango tree,
and lots of rocks.

Tiny Island was surrounded by water,
all alone.
Whale was alone too.
But she wasn't lonely.

Whale had friends on Tiny Island,
Lumpo, Bob, and Grumpy Gus.
Whale's friends were always
there for her, no matter what.

One day Whale invited her friends
to a tea party.
She set out her picnic blanket,
and everyone gathered around.

Whale made some sand dollar cookies.
They were a big hit.
"More tea?" asked Whale.
"Lumpo . . . ?
Bob . . . ?
Grumpy Gus . . . ?"

Whale sighed sadly.
It was nice to have friends.
But sometimes she wished
she had at least one friend
who wasn't a rock.

When the cookies were all gone,
Whale went to make some more.

It ended up taking quite a while.

When Whale finally returned,
something was different.

Lumpo was on his side.
Bob was upside down.
And someone was standing
on Grumpy Gus.
A new someone!

"Hi, I'm Quail," the someone said.
"Are you new here too?"
Whale shook her head.
"Is this a good island for exploring?"
asked Quail.
"Uhhh," said Whale, unsure.

"That's okay. I will go find out!"
said Quail.
Whale watched as Quail
explored Tiny Island.

"Look! This rock has a crack in it,"
said Quail.
"That's his mouth," said Whale.
"Rocks don't have mouths," said Quail.
"Grumpy Gus does. See?"
Whale said, and showed Quail
his frown.

"Lumpo has hair," said Whale.
"And Bob is just Bob."
Quail laughed and bounced away
to explore some more.

"You're probably too busy exploring
to come to my tea party,"
called Whale.
Quail turned and bounced back.
"I'm never too busy for tea!" she said.

Whale grinned.
Having a friend who was not a rock
was already better than she hoped
it would be.

Just then, Whale noticed something.
It looked like a rock.
A rock riding a wave . . .
and heading straight for the party!

"Hit the deck!" she yelled.

CRASH!
Whale opened her eyes.
"Oh no!" wailed Whale.
"That rock ruined everything!"

The rock stared back, then it spoke.
"Who are you calling a rock?
The name's Snail. See?" Snail said,
giving Whale their card.

"We thought you were a rock,"
said Quail.
"I get that a lot," said Snail.
"What is all this?"
"It's a tea party," said Quail.
"A party for me?" said Snail.
"That's more like it!"

"Actually, it's for my friends,"
said Whale.
"Friends? What friends?"
asked Snail, looking around.
"The ones you knocked over!" yelled
Whale.

Snail hid in their shell.

"I messed everything up," Snail said.

"It's okay, Snail," said Quail.

"Really?" asked Snail.

"Really?" asked Whale.

"It was an accident," said Quail. "Want to stay for tea?"

Snail peeked back out and nodded.
So while Quail showed Snail the island,
Whale poured a cup of tea for Snail.

"Where did you get these
awesome cookies?" asked Snail.
"I made them," said Whale.
"Wow!" said Snail.
"Got any more? Surfing works up
quite an appetite."
Whale nodded proudly.

"I'm glad you invited me to your tea party," Quail said.
"Me too," said Whale.

"I'm glad I'm not a rock!" said Snail,
eating more cookies.
"Rocks can't surf,
and they can't eat."

Whale laughed.
She loved having tea parties,
and she loved having friends.

Old friends who would always
be there for her
and two new friends
who were not rocks.

"Best day ever!" said Snail.
Whale and her friends all agreed.